My Favorite Shoes

J²B Publishing

My Favorite Shoes is dedicated to my wonderful hubby, Tom, of 54 years, and our three beautiful, smart and talented daughters, Tammy, Wendy and Kelby! Thanks for all of your encouragement and love!

– Linda

My Favorite Shoes

Text Copyright 2023 by Linda Dutrow
Images Copyright 2023 by Mary Barrows

All rights reserved. No part of this book may be reproduced or transmitted in any form or by any means, electronic or mechanical, including photocopying, or recording, or by any information storage and retrieval system without written permission from publisher or author. The only exception is brief quotations for review.

For information address:
J2B Publishing LLC
4251 Columbia Park Road
Pomfret, MD 20675

www.J2BLLC.com

ISBN - 978-1-954682-67-2

Printed and bound in the United States of America.

This book is set in Annie Use Your Telescope

Designed by Mary Barrows

My Favorite Shoes

By Linda Dutrow

Illustrated by Mary Barrows

Looking back upon my life
I find myself in thought
Through all the years
my love for shoes
I'd ever worn or bought!

In teeny-tiny little shoes
Was how I learned to toddle
With every teensy step I took
I balanced with a waddle...

Your grandpa got his camera out
And took a pose of me
Standing in my baby shoes
Beside our Christmas tree!

When I turned 6 and "so" grown up
Mom took me to the City
And bought me patent Mary Janes
That made me feel so pretty...

And I would wear them everywhere
Before and after school
Until one day with much surprise
Too small for me they grew!

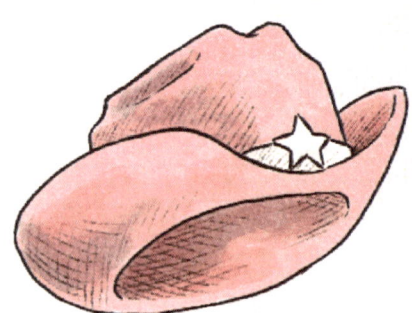

At seven, every Saturday
Rushed down the stairs I'd go
To eat my breakfast, brush my teeth
Then watch my *(favorite)* TV show...

In darling pink-stitched cowgirl boots
I'd sing along with them
"Happy Trails to You..."
Sang Roy and Dale
"Until we meet again!"

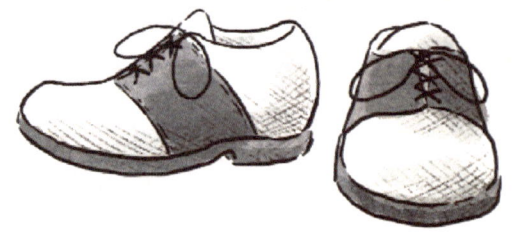

A little older I did turn
and wanted to impress
My bigger sister, Anna-Mae,
So like her I would dress...

And begged my mom to buy me ones
Just like my Anna-Mae
So black and white, my saddle shoes
I proudly wore each day!

But right before my birthday, 12th,
While skipping down the lane
It happened that I saw them through
The Woolworth window pane...

A pair of leather penny loafers
Smiled and looked at me
And then mom knew my birthday gift
Those lucky shoes should be!

The 60's rock and rolled the charts
The craze was fashion-flair
And just like every teenaged girl
I had to have a pair...

Of cool and swingin' Go-Go boots
I felt the "trendy-setter"
With Beatles, bangs and groovy things
Could life get any better?

Well, yes, it did –
I met my love
And on our wedding day
The gown, the veil, the ring I wore
For him were on display...

I'd never felt so beautiful
And in romantic style
In 3-inch lacey, lovely heels
Walked t'wards him down the aisle!

Pumps and wedgies topped the charts
Of 1980's fare
And just to keep up with the kids
I had to have (at least) a pair...

Comfy, soft and stylish, too,
It didn't matter when
My woven-wedgies, tan and pink
I'd wear... Then wear again!

I can't forget the mules I bought
In 90's they had thrived
The cloggy, clunky, slip-on phase
Had finally arrived...

I loved them, though, and wore a pair
With everything it seems...
I donned them proudly day or night
With pant-suits, skorts and jeans!

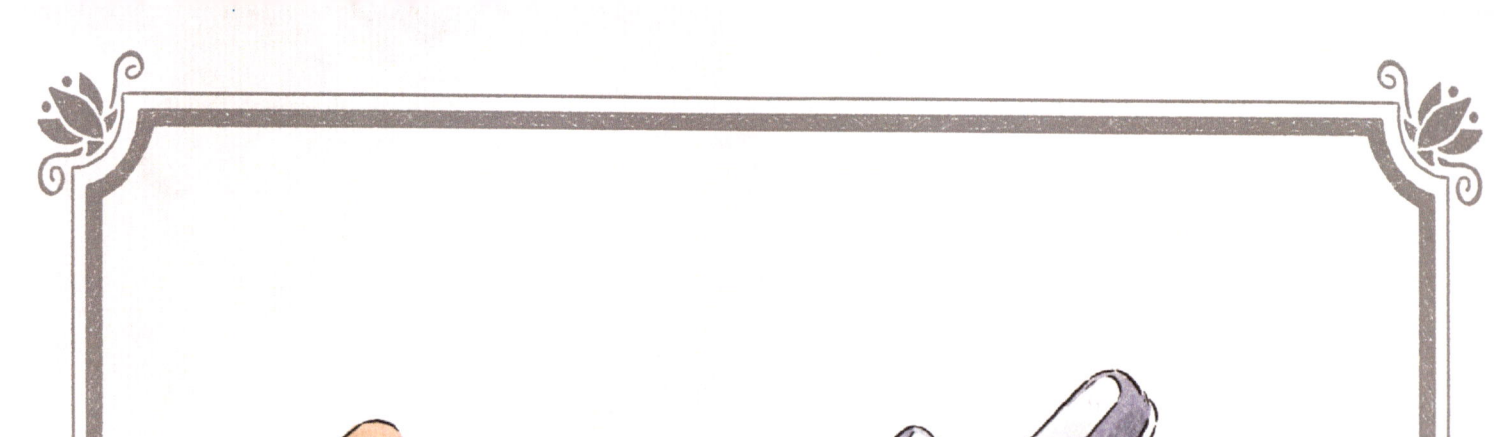

In Y2K I loved the flats
That molded round my toes
They felt so good I couldn't help
But buy a lot of those...

Red ones, yellow, blue and green
My closet burst in prism
With colors...
orange, chartreuse, mauve
To serve my "shoe-love-ism!"

Now in my 60's I did find
That sneakers were the craze
And helped to soothe my time-worn feet
To match my body's age...

I never thought I'd love them so
Until the aches and pains
Of wearing heels and clogs and boots
Left me with bursting veins!

It's funny, fluffy slippers now
I wear upon my feet
They look like two big panda paws
As I walk down the street...

And though some people laugh and stare
I'm sure what's really true
Is that they wish upon their feet
Were comfy bear paws, too!

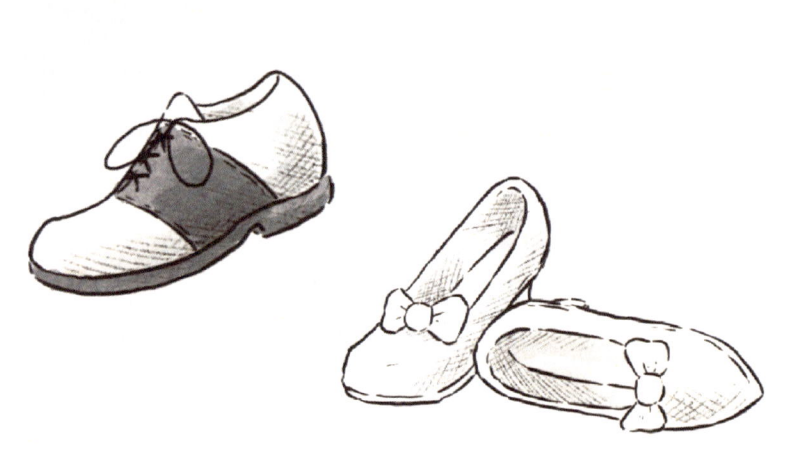

You've asked about my favorite shoes
In style that I most treasure
It's hard to pick the ones I loved
That gave me the most pleasure...

Except to say I'm older now
And forthright shall opine
That I can share quite openly
The favorite ones of mine!

Authentically original
They get me place to place
And honestly I have to say
My love for them embrace...

They're with me everywhere I go
And always within sight
While faithfully they serve my needs
Each morning, noon and night...

They may not be the prettiest
But won't turn obsolete...

My favorite pair
amongst them all...

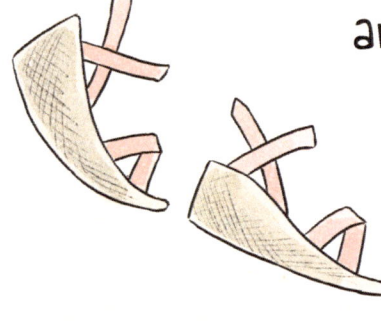

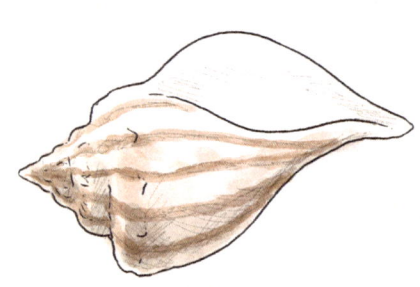

Are "just" my own two feet!

"Your" Favorite Shoes
(Draw, paste or insert pictures of "your" favorite shoes)

Linda Dutrow (aka Mimi Linny) - Now retired after 42 years of office management service with the City of Frederick, Maryland, Linda's life-long love of writing poetry has always been a fun way to capture stories, songs, holidays and life's adventures for family, friends and co-workers. Specializing in the strength of rhyme and rhythm, creativity and imagination, retirement has given her the opportunity to pursue this love of assembling the written word into poetic form.

Mary Barrows is a freelance illustrator from Maryland. Since she was old enough to hold a pencil, she has been drawing pictures of her favorite stories and she has not stopped yet. She works both digitally and traditionally using a variety of mediums in her work including: gouache, ink, watercolor, and colored pencil.

To contact visit: www.marybarrows.wordpress.com or via email at marybarrowsillustration@gmail.com

Printed in the USA
CPSIA information can be obtained
at www.ICGtesting.com
LVRC080114180224
772038LV00012B/162